MOUSE MAGIC

Books in the Animal Ark Pets series

BEN M. BAGLIO

MOUSE MAGIC

Illustrated by
Paul Howard

Cover Illustration by
Chris Chapman

A
LITTLE APPLE
PAPERBACK

SCHOLASTIC INC.
New York Toronto London Auckland Sydney
Mexico City New Delhi Hong Kong

Special thanks to Helen Magee.
Thanks also to C. J. Hall, B.Vet. Med., M.R.C.V.S., for reviewing
the veterinary material contained in this book.

ISBN 0-439-05162-2

Text copyright © 1996 by Ben M. Baglio.
Illustrations copyright © 1996 by Paul Howard.

All rights reserved. Published by Scholastic Inc.,
555 Broadway, New York, NY 10012, by arrangement with Hodder Headline.
SCHOLASTIC and associated logos are trademarks and/or registered
trademarks of Scholastic Inc.

12 11 10 9 8   1 2 3 4/0

Printed in the U.S.A.   40
First Scholastic trade paperback printing, August 1999

Contents

1

The Wizard of Welford

Mandy Hope ran down the road toward the low stone cottage where she lived. As she banged the garden gate shut behind her, the wooden sign above it swung in the breeze. Mandy looked up at the sign. It said ANIMAL ARK. She smiled. It was a great name for a vet's practice.

Mandy's face was flushed with excitement. She shook her short fair hair out of her eyes and ran on down the garden path. She burst through the front door and into the house.

"Mom!" she yelled, dumping her schoolbag on the floor of the hall. "Mom, guess what!"

Dr. Emily Hope came out of the door that led into the clinic at the end of the hall. There was another woman behind her.

"Hello, Jean," Mandy said. Jean Knox was the receptionist for Animal Ark.

"Somebody is in a rush," Jean said, smiling.

"Mandy," Dr. Emily said. "You're back early."

Mandy grinned at her mother and Jean. Dr. Emily's red curly hair was tied back neatly with a green scarf and she looked cool and calm in her white lab coat. Jean's hair was ruffled and her glasses dangled on the end of their cord around her neck.

"I ran all the way home from school," Mandy said, catching her breath.

Dr. Emily smiled. "Okay, what's the news?" she asked. "Come on, you can tell me while I

2

clean up. I've just got one or two more things to do in the residential unit."

"The school hall is finished," Mandy said, following her mother and Jean back through the door to the clinic.

Dr. Emily led the way to the residential unit. Mandy's parents were both vets in the little village of Welford. The residential unit was where animals were kept if they were still too sick to go home.

"The school hall?" asked Dr. Emily. "Is that what all the excitement is about?"

Mandy shook her head. "It isn't just that," she said. "Mrs. Garvie says we can put on a play to celebrate — like a special opening ceremony. We started the auditions today."

Mrs. Garvie was the principal of Welford Elementary School.

"That sounds exciting," said Dr. Emily.

The telephone rang in the reception room.

"Don't tell all the news before I get back," called Jean as she went to answer it.

Mandy watched as her mother unhooked

one of the rows of cages that lined the residential unit and brought out a tiny kitten. One of his legs was wrapped in plaster.

Mandy leaned forward eagerly. "Is Snowy all right now?" she asked anxiously.

Dr. Emily nodded. "He will be fine in a few days," she said. She tapped the kitten lightly on the nose. "And let's hope he won't go climbing trees again until he's a lot older."

"And able to get back down!" Mandy said, smiling. "Susan will be pleased."

Snowy belonged to Susan Davis. She was older and went to Welford Village School and Snowy was her very first pet. He had climbed up a tree in Susan's garden and got stuck. Then he'd tried to jump down and had broken his leg.

Dr. Emily put Snowy back in his cage and turned to Mandy.

"Now, tell me all about this play," she said.

Mandy clapped a hand to her mouth.

"Oh, I forgot about that for a minute," she said.

Dr. Emily shook her head and laughed. "You always forget about everything else when there's an animal to be looked after."

"You can say that again," said Jean, coming into the residential unit with a pile of forms.

Mandy grinned. "But animals are so *important*," she said. "And anyway, that's just it. Mrs. Garvie says we can have some animals in the play — only really well-behaved ones, of course."

Dr. Emily nodded. "I knew your news

would have something to do with animals," she said. "Nothing else gets you this excited, Mandy."

"Performing animals!" Jean said, putting the pile of forms down in front of Snowy's cage. "Whatever next?"

Mandy smiled. "Oh, it's going to be wonderful," she said. "Just imagine, Mom. A school play with animals in it — isn't it terrific? Is Dad home? I want to tell him all about it, too."

Dr. Emily looked at her watch. "He should be home for dinner," she said. "He's doing evening clinic hours later. Let me get cleaned up here and sign these forms for Jean. Then I'll start making dinner."

"Can I help clean up?" Mandy said. Mandy loved helping out in the residential unit, even if it was just cleaning the counters. Her parents wouldn't let her actually help with the animals yet. She had to wait until she was twelve. Three whole years!

Dr. Emily handed her a bottle of disinfectant and a disposable cloth.

"Don't forget the corners," she said. "That's where the germs are."

"I won't," said Mandy, already starting work.

She scooped up a pile of forms from in front of Snowy's cage. The little kitten had one paw through the bars and was steadily edging the papers off the counter.

"Something tells me that kitten is going to be quite a handful when he grows up," said Dr. Emily, laughing. "You'd better give those to me, Mandy."

By the time Mandy had cleaned all the counters — and talked to all the animals — Dr. Emily had finished giving medicine to the animals and signed all the forms.

"Oh," said Mandy, "I forgot. James is coming for dinner. Is that all right? He's got some extra special news about the play."

Dr. Emily smiled. "James is always welcome," she said. "You go and get changed."

"I'll just file these and then get going," said Jean, collecting the forms. "Put my name down for a ticket for the play, Mandy."

"I will," Mandy promised. "I'll get you a seat in the very front row!"

Mandy changed into jeans and a T-shirt quickly. She heard her father's deep voice as she came downstairs into the kitchen.

"Look who I found outside," said Dr. Adam Hope, his dark eyes twinkling.

"James!" said Mandy, looking at the boy standing beside her dad. He had floppy brown hair and glasses that were halfway down his nose. A young black Labrador fidgeted beside him.

James Hunter was a year younger than Mandy. He was her best friend. His Labrador gave a short bark and launched himself at Mandy on his long, gangly legs. Mandy giggled and rubbed his ears.

"Oh, Blackie," she said. "Have you come for dinner, too?"

James blushed. "I tried to make him stay at home," he said.

"That's all right," Dr. Adam said, laughing. "After all, this *is* Animal Ark."

"As if we wouldn't want to see Blackie," Mandy said. "Come on, James, let's set the table. Then we can tell all our news."

"Salad tonight," Dr. Emily said, going to the refrigerator.

Mandy and James set the big pine table that was in the middle of the kitchen while Dr. Emily took bowls of salad, hard-boiled eggs, and quiche from the refrigerator.

"That looks good," said Dr. Adam as they all sat down. "Now, what's this news?"

James and Mandy began to speak at once and Dr. Adam held up his hand. "One at a time," he said.

Mandy started to tell her dad all about the school hall and the play.

"The play is going to be called *The Wizard of Welford*," she said.

"It's all about a wizard who comes to Welford and shows people how smart animals are," said James.

"And there's a bad character," said Mandy. "Horrible Horace. Andrew Pearson is going to play him because he's the tallest boy in school."

"Horace is really mean to animals and the wizard has to find a way to show him how cruel he is," said James.

"Only we haven't got that part right yet," Mandy said.

"We've been working on the story all day at school," James said.

"Gary Roberts wants to frighten Horrible Horace with Gertie," Mandy said.

Dr. Adam laughed. "Gertie is only a garter snake," he said. "It doesn't sound as though she'll be enough to frighten Horrible Horace."

James nodded. "That's what the rest of us said," he replied. "So Gary is going to be a snake charmer in the play instead."

"Maybe he could put a spell on Horrible Horace," Dr. Emily suggested.

Mandy shook her head. "Snake charmers only put spells on snakes," she said. "What we need is a special spell for the wizard to put on Horrible Horace."

"You'll think of something," Dr. Adam said.

Mandy nodded. "I hope so," she said. "We also need a better ending for the play."

"And when we think of it, we'll keep it a surprise," said James. "We won't tell anyone before the play."

Mandy grinned. "*If* we think of something," she said. "But the really terrific news is about the wizard." She turned to James. "Tell them!"

James blushed. "You tell them," he mumbled, pushing his glasses up on his nose.

Mandy turned to her parents. "James is going to be the wizard!" she said.

"Congratulations, James," said Dr. Emily warmly.

James blushed even more. "I've got to learn to do magic tricks," he said. "I got a book out of the school library but it looks difficult. I'll need to practice really hard. Did Mandy tell you she's got a part, too?"

"Oops!" said Mandy to her parents. "I was so

busy telling you about the animals I forgot. I'm the wizard's apprentice."

"Very nice, Mandy," Dr. Emily said. "I'm sure you and James will make a great team."

"The Wizard of Welford," Dr. Adam said. "Maybe you can put a spell on Blackie."

Mandy and James looked at the black Labrador. Blackie was lying in the corner of the kitchen quietly chewing one of Dr. Adam's slippers.

"Blackie!" James yelled, making a dive for him.

"Uh-oh," said Mandy. "If Blackie is quiet it always means he's up to something."

Blackie looked up and put his head to one

side. The slipper dangled from his mouth. His big dark eyes looked innocent.

Dr. Emily laughed. "I think it would take more than a wizard to train Blackie," she said.

James got the slipper away from Blackie and held it up. "It's all chewed up, Dr. Adam," he said.

"It's about time Mandy's dad got a new pair of slippers anyway," Dr. Emily said. "I've been trying to get rid of those for ages. You've done me a big favor, James. In fact, it's magic!"

"You see," said Mandy. "It's working already. James really *is* a wizard!"

2
Mr. Spellini

"You'll need a wizard's costume," Mandy said to James as they helped clear away the dishes.

"You mean like a pointy hat and a cloak?" said James.

Mandy nodded. "A cloak with things like stars and moons on it," she said.

"Why don't you ask Grandma to help?" Dr.

Emily said. "You know how good she is at things like that."

"Great," Mandy said. "I was going to talk to her about my costume anyway. Let's go now, James."

Dr. Adam stacked a pile of plates in the sink. "See if you can come up with a spell that makes dishes wash themselves, James," he said.

Mandy grinned. "Is that a hint for us to help with the dishes?" she asked.

Dr. Emily turned the water on. "No, it isn't," she said. "Off you go!"

"Come on, Blackie," Mandy said.

Blackie leaped up and galloped to the door.

"Abracadabra!" Dr. Adam said to the pile of plates, waving the scrub brush.

Mandy laughed and shot out of the door with James and Blackie.

"See you later," she called back.

Mandy's grandma and grandpa lived at Lilac Cottage, not far from Animal Ark. Mandy and James passed Hobart's Corner on the way.

Mandy looked through the gates at the house as they passed. The windows and the fresh white paint shone in the evening light. The garden was full of flowers and the grass had been newly mowed.

"Hobart's Corner is really looking great now," she said.

James nodded. "I always thought it looked spooky," he admitted. "But only because it was empty for so long."

Jack Gardiner and his parents had moved into the house at Hobart's Corner two months ago. They were turning it into a guest house. Jack was seven and had a pet rabbit named Hoppy.

"I wonder how Hoppy is," Mandy said.

"We could go and visit him," said James.

Mandy shook her head. "Maybe later. Let's see about your costume first."

They found Grandma and Grandpa in the back garden of Lilac Cottage. Grandpa was working in his vegetable patch and Grandma was picking strawberries. Mandy's grandpa was a champion vegetable grower.

"Hi, Grandma! Hi, Grandpa!" Mandy called as she and James came through the gate.

Grandpa looked up as Blackie bounded over to him.

"Hello, young fellow," Grandpa said, giving Blackie a pat.

"You two are just in time," Grandma said to Mandy and James. "Come and help me pick some strawberries."

Mandy and James grinned. Their favorite task!

"Three for the basket and one for the picker," Mandy said.

Grandma smiled. "That's the best way to pick them."

Mandy and James took a basket each from the garage and started picking.

"Grandma," said Mandy, "James and I wanted to ask you a favor."

"Oh!" said Grandpa. "You've found a stray puppy and you want us to take it in."

Mandy looked at Blackie. The Labrador

was lying contentedly on the ground while Grandpa tickled his tummy.

"No," she said. "We want Grandma to make a costume for James, please. And one for me, if she's got time."

Mandy explained all about the play while she and James and Grandma worked their way down the row of strawberries. The fruit smelled sweet. Mandy finished explaining and popped a plump, juicy fruit into her mouth.

"Mmm," she said. "These are delicious!"

"Let's go inside and you can have a bowl of them with some cream," Grandma said. "Your costume should be easy enough, Mandy. A tunic would do. But we should try out some designs for James's costume."

"So, you'll do it?" said James.

Grandma smiled. "I'd love to make a wizard's costume," she said.

"And I'd love some strawberries and cream," Grandpa said, leaning on his hoe. "Gardening is hard work."

Mandy laughed as they all trooped inside.

Grandma got some paper and pencils and they all sat around the kitchen table with their bowls of fruit, discussing James's costume.

"That was great," said Mandy, scraping up the last of the cream with her spoon.

"And just look at the design for my costume," James said. Mandy looked at the sheet of paper in front of Grandma. She had drawn a long flowing cloak covered with stars and moons.

"I'll use silver paper for the decorations," Grandma said. "And plenty of sequins."

"I'll make you a long black mustache, James," said Grandpa. "It'll make you look mysterious."

"And we'll need a hat," said Mandy. "James and I can make one from black oak tag and stick more sequins on it."

"Now, about your costume, Mandy," Grandma said. "What exactly do you have to do in the play? Do you need to be able to run around?"

Mandy grinned. "Oh, yes! I'm the wizard's apprentice," she said. "I've got to set the bravest dog in the village on Horrible Horace to save my master."

"Guess who the dog is," said James.

"Don't tell us — Blackie," said Grandpa.

James nodded. "Mrs. Garvie asked for him specially."

Blackie looked up and gave a short bark.

"The only trouble will be training him to *stop* chasing Andrew Pearson," Mandy said, giving Blackie's ears a rub.

"Blackie has to get the wizard's wand back when Horrible Horace steals it," said James. "It's a very important part in the play. The wizard is powerless without his wand."

"We're going to try and include all the pets we can," said Mandy. "It's going to be wonderful."

"Jill Redfern is going to bring Toto, her tortoise," said James.

"And then there's Duchess, Richard Tanner's Persian cat," said Mandy.

"And Laura Baker's rabbits," said James. "And Amy Fenton is going to do some gymnastics. She's really excited."

"Amy was upset that Minnie can't have a part," Mandy explained. "But Mrs. Garvie couldn't see how we could fit a mouse into the story."

"That's why Amy is doing some gymnastics instead," James said.

"Is Jack Gardiner's rabbit, Hoppy, going to be in the play?" Grandma asked.

James nodded. "Mmm. We're going to go and see Jack on the way home," he said.

"And Hoppy," Mandy added.

"Don't get in the way," Grandma said. "Mrs. Gardiner is expecting her very first paying guest today and she's really excited. She wants everything to be just right. They've worked so hard getting Hobart's Corner fixed up."

"We won't get in the way," said Mandy, getting up from the table. "Thanks for the strawberries, Grandma."

"And for agreeing to make the costume and the mustache," said James.

"Come on, Blackie," Mandy said. "Let's go and see if Mrs. Gardiner's paying guest has brought a pet."

Mandy and James found Jack playing with Hoppy in the garden at Hobart's Corner. The black-and-white rabbit looked up at them with his bright black eyes. He wasn't at all afraid of Mandy and James. He knew them very well.

"Hi, Hoppy!" Mandy said, tickling the little animal behind the ears.

Hoppy sat up on his hind legs and began to wash his whiskers. Jack held out a lettuce leaf and Hoppy sniffed at it, then nibbled delicately.

"He's getting so big," Mandy said.

Jack stretched out a hand and stroked his rabbit. "Laura says he's even bigger than Patch," he said.

Laura Baker had three rabbits — Nibbles, Fluffy, and Patch. Patch was from the same litter as Hoppy. Jack didn't want a pet when he first came to Welford, but as soon as he saw Fluffy's babies being born he fell in love with them. So Laura had asked him if he wanted one and Jack had chosen Hoppy.

"Grandma says you're getting your first paying guest," said Mandy. "Do you know who it is?"

Jack shook his head. "He should be arriving any time. I'm watching for him. Mom says his name is Mr. Spellini. But she doesn't know anything else about him."

"What an odd name," said James.

Mandy heard a car pull up at the gate and turned quickly.

"It's a taxi," said James. "It must be him."

Mandy, James, and Jack watched as the taxi turned into the driveway and stopped at the front door.

"Can you see him?" asked Jack.

"Wait a minute. He's getting out," Mandy said.

They watched as a tall thin man stepped out of the taxi. He stood for a moment, looking around the garden. Mandy drew in her breath. He looked extraordinary. He was wearing a long black cape and he had a top hat on. Mandy could see he had very dark eyes and a pointed black beard. He was carrying what looked like two big covered boxes with handles on top. He put them down very carefully on the front steps of the house.

"Wow!" James gulped. "Look at those clothes."

"They are strange!" said Mandy. "I wonder what's in the boxes."

Jack's eyes were large, round saucers.

Mr. Spellini walked to the back of the taxi as the driver opened the trunk. He reached in and lifted out a big black trunk. He put the trunk on the ground and the taxi drove off. Then he looked around the garden — and saw them.

Mandy felt her eyes popping as he swept off his top hat and bowed to them. His cape swirled about him. Then he turned and disappeared into the house.

"Wow!" said James. "Who do you think he is?"

Mandy was looking at the trunk. It was very big and very black and it had a huge lock on it.

"And what do you think is in the trunk?" she asked.

"I don't know," James said. "But I've never seen anybody like Mr. Spellini before."

3

Magic at the Store

For the next few days, Mandy and James were really busy rehearsing the play. On Friday afternoon they were onstage in the middle of more rehearsals. All the children were there. James brought Blackie so that they could rehearse his part. Mrs. Todd and Mrs. Black, James's, and Mandy's teachers, were in charge.

James was still thinking about the mysterious Mr. Spellini and his locked trunk. Jack hadn't found out what was in it and James's imagination was running wild.

"Maybe Mr. Spellini's got a body stashed away in the trunk," he said, rolling his eyes dramatically so that his glasses slid right down his nose.

"Or stacks of money from a bank robbery," said Mandy.

"Shh! Here comes Mrs. Garvie," warned Jill Redfern behind them.

"You've all done very well so far," said Mrs. Garvie as she came up on to the stage. "But I want you to practice hard all next week as well. The big day is a week from Saturday and I want everything perfect for then."

"I'll never get Gertie ready by then," said Gary Roberts.

Mrs. Garvie gave him a weary look. "It isn't Gertie you need to worry about, Gary," she said. "What you need to do is practice your part on the recorder."

Everybody laughed. Gary wasn't very good at playing the recorder.

"I'm getting very good at being Horrible Horace," Andrew Pearson said. He growled at little Laura Baker. "Get out of my way or your rabbits will end up in a rabbit pie," he snarled.

"Huh!" said Laura. "You'll have to do better than that. Even Patch wouldn't be frightened of *that* and Fluffy would probably bite you."

"How are your magic tricks coming along, James?" Mrs. Garvie asked.

James bit his lip. "Not very well, Mrs. Garvie," he said. "It's really hard to learn tricks from a book."

"I'm sure you'll manage with practice," said Mrs. Garvie. "Mandy can help you."

"We're going to get some playing cards from the store," Mandy said. "Card tricks might not be so difficult."

Mrs. Garvie looked at Blackie sitting at James's feet. "And how's Blackie doing with his part?"

Blackie had to chase Horrible Horace

31

around the stage. Then Horrible Horace had to throw the wizard's wand away and Blackie had to retrieve it and bring it to Mandy.

"He's very good at the chasing part," Mandy said.

"That's true," Andrew said. "He wouldn't stop chasing me last time we practiced. And when he retrieved the wand, he brought it back to me instead of taking it to Mandy."

"That's because he's trained to give the stick back to whoever throws it," said James.

"Oh, I've got an idea that should solve that," said Mandy. She held up a packet of dog biscuits.

"What are those for?" said Andrew.

"I'm going to try rattling the dog biscuits when he retrieves the wand," she said. "I bet Blackie would rather have a biscuit than come back to you with a stick, Andrew."

"That's a good idea," said Mrs. Garvie.

Andrew didn't look convinced.

"At least Blackie's got a part," Amy Fenton said. "Poor Minnie hasn't got a part at all."

Mrs. Garvie shook her head. "It's a little difficult to think of a part for a white mouse," she said. "And I wouldn't want Duchess to scare her."

Duchess, Richard Tanner's Persian cat, was huge. She would scare the life out of Minnie.

"At least I can do my gymnastics," Amy said as Mrs. Garvie went to speak to another group of pupils. "But I'm still sorry for poor Minnie."

Mandy smiled at her. "Why don't you ask Mrs. Garvie if you can bring Minnie to the pets rehearsal next week? As long as you keep her in her cage Duchess won't harm her."

Amy cheered up. "That's a good idea," she said. "I'll do that. She'd like to see the play."

"Now back to work," Mrs. Todd said. "We've still got a lot to do. Let's try Blackie's part — with the dog biscuits this time."

Andrew took his place center stage as the villagers cowered in fear before him. James lay down at Mandy's feet.

Mandy put her hand lightly on Blackie's collar, keeping him close to her. Then she turned to Andrew.

"Look what you have done to my master!" she cried. "You have stolen his wand. You have stolen his power!"

Andrew raised the wizard's magic wand.

"And now I'm going to turn all your pets to stone," he snarled.

Mandy dropped to one knee and gave Blackie a little push. "Go, Blackie," she said urgently. "Get Andrew!"

Blackie trotted forward and Andrew threw his hands in the air and began to run away from the dog. Once, twice, three times around the stage. Then Andrew flung the wand high in the air. Blackie looked up. He watched the stick turn and twist as it fell toward him. He made a leap and caught it.

Quickly Mandy pulled out the packet of dog biscuits and rattled them. Blackie's ears pricked as he heard the familiar sound. He turned and looked at Mandy.

"Here, boy," she whispered.

Blackie ran toward her and Mandy grabbed the wand and gave Blackie his reward. Blackie crunched the biscuit as the rest of the cast started to clap.

"It worked," said Mrs. Garvie. "Great job, Mandy!"

Mandy smiled. "Good boy, Blackie," she said to the Labrador.

By the time school was over, Mandy and

James were very proud of Blackie. James clipped on the Labrador's leash as they walked through the school gates.

"You were great, boy," he said, giving Blackie a pat.

Mandy laughed. "I think the dog biscuits helped," she said.

"One thing's for sure," James said. "Blackie is going to really like rehearsing now that he knows he gets biscuits as a reward."

"I'll just have to make sure he doesn't get too many," Mandy said, "or he'll get fat."

"Let's see if Mrs. McFarlane has those playing cards I need for my magic tricks," James said as they reached the store.

"Mrs. McFarlane has everything," Mandy said as they pushed open the door and went in.

The general store was their favorite shop in the village. It sold all kinds of things — comics and candy, games and books. Mandy was so busy looking at the animal magazines by the door that she didn't notice when James suddenly stopped dead.

"Ouch!" she said, bumping into him. "What's the matter?"

"Look!" James said. "It's *him*."

Mandy looked across at the store counter. Mr. Spellini, the mysterious guest at Hobart's Corner, was buying stamps, his black cape thrown over one shoulder. Mrs. McFarlane looked over to Mandy and James and smiled.

"I'll be a minute," she said.

"That's all right, Mrs. McFarlane," Mandy said. "We'll just have a look around. James is looking for playing cards."

"I have to learn some magic tricks," James explained with a grin.

"You'll find them on the far wall, bottom shelf," Mrs. McFarlane said and turned back to the counter.

As James walked over to search for them, Mandy saw Mr. Spellini turning to look at them. He seemed very interested in what they were doing. Then her attention was caught by a shelf of toys in the corner of the shop and she forgot all about him.

"Hey, James," she called, picking up a box from the shelf. "Look what I've found."

James came over, a pack of playing cards in his hand.

"Magic tricks!" he said, reading the label on the box. "These look terrific."

The bell on the door rang as a large woman with a hat perched right on top of her head came bustling into the shop. She carried an overweight Pekingese under one arm.

It was Mrs. Ponsonby, the bossiest woman in Welford. Blackie galloped over and tried to make friends with the Pekingese, but it only yapped at him.

"Good afternoon, Mandy," Mrs. Ponsonby said. Then, before Mandy could reply, she caught sight of James with the pack of cards in his hand.

"Playing cards!" she said. "James Hunter, I hope you are not taking to gambling!"

James tried to say something, but Mrs. Ponsonby paid no attention.

"And what else do you have there?" she

asked, peering at the box in his other hand. "Magic tricks! What a waste of money! You should be buying something educational instead of spending money on tricks."

Mandy saw someone move out of the corner of her eye. She looked around. Mr. Spellini turned from the store counter, his black cape swirling around him. For a moment he looked straight at Mandy. His eyes sparkled and he gave her a wink. Then he swept up to Mrs. Ponsonby and bowed.

"You do not like magic tricks, madam?" he said.

Mrs. Ponsonby looked startled. "I don't like surprises," she said. "Not that any trick could surprise me. I'm not easily taken in, you know."

Mr. Spellini spread his hands wide. "Are you never surprised?" he said. "Not even when you find something strange behind your ear?"

"Behind my ear?" Mrs. Ponsonby screeched. "What on earth are you talking about?"

Mr. Spellini smiled widely and stretched out

his hand. Before Mrs. Ponsonby could say another word, Mr. Spellini put his hand behind
her ear and drew out an egg.

"Wow!" said James, his mouth dropping
open. "Did you see that?"

"How did he do it?" said Mandy.

"Magic!" James breathed.

Mrs. Ponsonby's eyes popped. "Where did
you get that?" she said, staring at the egg in Mr.
Spellini's hand.

Mr. Spellini smiled. "From behind your ear,"
he said. He put his head to one side. "A sur-
prising place to keep an egg."

And, with another bow, he swept out of the
shop, his cape billowing behind him.

"Well!" said Mrs. Ponsonby at last. "Did you
ever see anything as rude as that in your life?
An egg behind my ear!"

Mandy and James stood there, their mouths
clamped shut, trying not to laugh.

Mrs. McFarlane's eyes were as round as
saucers.

"Well," she said, "I must say that Mr. Spellini

is a strange one. You don't see many top hats and capes in Welford, and as for taking eggs out of people's ears, I've never seen anything like it!"

"Hmmph," said Mrs. Ponsonby. "If you ask me there's something funny about that man. Anybody that goes around in a big black cape just has to be suspicious. I think he's a spy."

"A spy?" said Mrs. McFarlane. "Why on earth would a spy come to Welford?"

"On a secret mission," Mrs. Ponsonby said. Mandy and James looked at each other.

"A secret mission?" Mandy whispered. "Mrs. Ponsonby must read some pretty weird books."

"If she thinks spies dress like that she must," James replied. "Mr. Spellini isn't a spy. He's a magician!"

4

The Mystery Trunk

Mandy and James paid for their things while Mrs. Ponsonby went on and on about spies. Poor Mrs. McFarlane couldn't get a word in. Mrs. Ponsonby was still talking as they made their escape.

"Did you see Mrs. Ponsonby's face?" James

said, whooping with laughter as they left the store.

"I thought she was going to explode," said Mandy. She could hardly walk because she was laughing so hard. "An egg! Oh, I wish I'd had a camera."

"And she thinks he's a spy," said James. "Anybody can see he's a magician."

Mandy looked thoughtful. "I wonder if Jack knows that," she said. "Let's go along to Hobart's Corner and see what we can find out."

"About Mr. Spellini?" James asked.

Mandy nodded. "*We'll* be the spies," she said, grinning.

They didn't get as far as the garden gates at Hobart's Corner. Halfway along the high garden wall Mandy stopped and looked around.

"Did you hear something?" she said.

James shook his head. Then the sound came again.

"Psst!" said a voice above their heads.

Mandy and James looked up. Jack was sprawled along the top of the garden wall.

"What are you doing up there?" said James.

Jack's face was lit up with excitement. "I've found out what's in Mr. Spellini's trunk," he exclaimed. "It's amazing! Come and see."

James headed for the gate, but Jack called him back.

"Up here, on the wall," the little boy said. "I've got a great view."

Mandy and James scrambled up the wall and perched beside Jack.

"What about Blackie?" asked Mandy, looking down at the Labrador.

Blackie looked up at her and scampered off in the direction of the gate.

"Blackie!" Mandy called softly but he paid no attention to her.

"Wow!" said James. "Look at that, Mandy."

Mandy looked where James was pointing. There was an apple tree right next to the wall and she had to twist around to see through the leaves. Then she saw why Jack was so excited.

Mr. Spellini was standing in the middle of the garden. There were two empty cages at his feet. One of them looked like a birdcage. The big black trunk stood wide open on the grass in front of him.

"He must have animals and birds," Mandy said softly. "Those boxes were really pet cages."

"He's got a rabbit," Jack said. "He bought a hutch from the pet shop in Walton for it and Dad's put it beside Hoppy's hutch. He's got doves, too, but he keeps them in that big birdcage in his room."

As they watched, Mr. Spellini took a little table out of the trunk and set it on the grass. He took out a vase, then waved his hands in the air. Suddenly he was holding a bunch of flowers. He popped the flowers into the vase and put the vase on the table.

Mandy gasped with delight. "Where did they come from?" she said.

"I wish I could learn to do that for the play," James said.

"Isn't he great?" said Jack, his eyes shining.

Mr. Spellini started to pull a long string of

colored flags out of his mouth and draped them across the table.

"Did you see what he did with those flags?" said James. "It must take years to learn how to do that."

Then Mr. Spellini took off his top hat — and pulled out a rabbit! He set the rabbit on the table in front of him beside the flowers. The little animal settled down comfortably and began to clean its whiskers.

"Look! That's his rabbit," said Jack, delighted.

"But where are the doves?" Mandy said.

At that moment Blackie came dashing through the garden gate and raced across the grass. Mr. Spellini picked up the rabbit — and it disappeared. He threw his hands in the air and four white doves fluttered into the sky. Blackie stopped and looked up. Then he started chasing the doves across the garden.

Mr. Spellini turned around and bowed to them.

"He's seen us," said Jack.

Mr. Spellini waved his hands twice in the air and the doves came fluttering back and settled on his arms. One of them picked its way delicately up his sleeve and sat on the magician's shoulder.

"You can come down now," Mr. Spellini called to them. "I hope you enjoyed the little show."

Mandy, James, and Jack scrambled down from the wall.

"We weren't really spying on you," said James, blushing.

Mr. Spellini laughed. "It's all right," he said, walking toward them. "I knew Jack was there and I thought I would give him a treat."

"That was great, Mr. Spellini," Jack said.

"Uh-oh!" said James as Blackie ran across the grass toward them.

Mr. Spellini gathered the doves together and put them into the birdcage, closing the door very gently. Then he hung the cage on a branch of the apple tree, well out of Blackie's reach.

"Oh, they're beautiful," Mandy breathed, looking at the doves. The birds ruffled their soft white feathers and settled down.

"How do you train them?" James asked.

Mr. Spellini waved his hand over the birds. A river of corn fell from his fingers and dropped into the cage.

"With kindness and rewards," he said. "It's the only way to train animals."

"I wish you could teach me a thing or two about training animals," James said, collaring Blackie.

Mr. Spellini stroked his beard. "And perhaps magic tricks as well?"

James looked up at the magician, his mouth open.

Mr. Spellini turned to Mandy. "When I saw you in the store you said James had to learn some magic tricks," he said.

Mandy nodded. "We're putting on a school play," she said. "James is going to be the Wizard of Welford. He has to do tricks. We're going to have some animals in the play as well."

Mr. Spellini smiled. "And when is this play?" he said.

James bit his lip. "Next Saturday," he said. "We don't have much time."

Mr. Spellini shook his head. "What you need is a little bit of magic," he said.

Mandy smiled. "Would you help us, Mr. Spellini?" she asked.

Mr. Spellini bowed. "I'd be delighted," he said. "It will be useful for me, too. A magician has to practice, you know. Even when he is on vacation."

"That would be great," James said.

Mr. Spellini looked at Jack, who had a puzzled frown on his face. "What do you think, Jack?" he said.

"I was wondering about the rabbit," he said. "The one that disappeared."

Mr. Spellini laughed and reached under his cape. He brought out the rabbit and handed it to Jack.

"You see," he said. "He's perfectly safe and well."

Jack cuddled the rabbit and looked up at Mr. Spellini. "There are rabbits in the play," he said. "I'm sure you'll like them."

"I'm sure I will, too," said Mr. Spellini. "But we must get to work if James is to turn into a wizard by next Saturday. That will take a lot of magic."

Mandy looked at Mr. Spellini. "Oh, you can do it," she said. "I just know you can."

5

Disaster

The first thing Mr. Spellini wanted to see was James's costume. He would not explain to Mandy why it was so important, but just looked mysterious. After that, of course, he wanted to meet Mrs. Garvie and get her permission to help.

Mandy and James arranged to take Mr.

Spellini to Lilac Cottage after dinner so that he could see Grandma's design for James's costume. Back at Animal Ark, Mandy was so excited she could hardly eat her meal, because she was talking about Mr. Spellini.

Dr. Emily phoned Jack's mother and came back all smiles.

"Mr. Spellini has been showing the Gardiners his scrapbook," she said. "He's quite famous, you know."

"I think he's wonderful," said Mandy.

"He was also asking about a vet," said Dr. Emily. "One of his doves is not eating so I've promised to go over and have a look at it. I'll drive you all to Grandma and Grandpa's afterwards."

"Maybe Mr. Spellini will show you some tricks," Mandy said. Then she frowned. "I hope the dove isn't sick."

When Mandy and Dr. Emily arrived at Hobart's Corner, Mr. Spellini was too concerned about his dove to do tricks for them. Mandy could see by his worried face that he really loved his animals.

Dr. Emily took the bird expertly in her hands. She ran her fingers carefully over its breast and up toward its throat. Then she pressed gently on each side of the dove's neck and watched as the bird tried to swallow.

"What's her name, Mr. Spellini?" Mandy asked.

The magician was watching Dr. Emily intently. "Bianca," he said without taking his eyes off her.

Dr. Emily finished examining Bianca and frowned slightly.

"There seems to be something in her throat," she said. "I'll have to take her into Animal Ark and have a closer look."

Mr. Spellini nodded and got a traveling cage for the dove.

"Bianca is a very clever bird," he said, closing the latch of the cage carefully. "I'd be lost without her."

Dr. Emily smiled. "I imagine she's a very valuable bird as well," she said.

Mr. Spellini nodded. "She is very special."

Dr. Emily took the cage gently from him. "I'm sure she'll be fine, Mr. Spellini," she said. "I'll be able to let you know how she is once I've examined her more thoroughly."

Mr. Spellini nodded again, but Mandy could see he was still worried as they all got into the car.

Dr. Emily picked up James and then drove them all to Lilac Cottage.

As they walked down the path toward the cottage, Grandma came out the front door.

"Grandma," said Mandy, "this is Mr. Spellini. He's a magician and he's going to help James with some magic tricks."

Grandma looked at Mr. Spellini and her face lit up.

"The Spectacular Spellini!" she said. "I saw you last year in York. You were very good."

Mr. Spellini bowed, drew a colored scarf

magically from between his fingers, and presented it to Grandma.

"Well," said Grandma, "it certainly must be very useful being a magician. I'm always losing scarves. It would be nice to conjure one up just like that when I needed it."

Mandy smiled, but she was still thinking about Bianca.

"Are you sure she'll be all right?" she whispered to her mother.

Dr. Emily smiled reassuringly. "Don't worry. It's probably just something stuck in her throat."

They followed Grandma indoors and soon Mr. Spellini was examining James's costume inside and out. "As I thought," he said. "Not enough pockets." He looked at James. "Magicians need lots of pockets."

Grandma, James, and Mr. Spellini went into a huddle over the costume while Grandpa brought a selection of fresh vegetables in from the garden for Dr. Emily.

"You don't get those by waving a magic wand!" Dr. Emily said.

Grandpa scratched his head. "It's a different kind of magic, getting things to grow," he said.

At last Mr. Spellini was satisfied with the new design for the costume and Dr. Emily drove him back to Hobart's Corner.

"Come at about eight o'clock this evening," she said. "You'll be able to see Bianca then."

Mr. Spellini said he would, but as they drove off, Mandy could see he was still very concerned.

Back at Animal Ark, Mandy hung around outside the room used as an operating room while Dr. Emily examined Bianca. Simon, the veterinary nurse for the practice, was on hand to help.

It seemed like hours before Simon poked his head outside. "All over now," he said, smiling at Mandy.

She hurried inside.

"You can stop worrying now," said her mother. "Bianca had a large seed stuck deep down in her throat. I removed it while she was asleep. She'll feel a bit sore for a little while, but she'll be all better in a day or two."

Mandy walked over to the operating table and looked down at the beautiful white dove just beginning to stir. Her eyelids fluttered slightly.

"We'll keep her in overnight," Dr. Emily said, "and she'll be able to go home tomorrow."

"And will she really be all right?" said Mandy.

"She'll be the star of Mr. Spellini's next show, you wait and see," Dr. Emily said.

Mandy smiled. She would have good news for Mr. Spellini.

When Mr. Spellini arrived he was full of thanks and very relieved to see Bianca looking well again.

"Mom says she'll be the star of the show again in no time," Mandy said to him.

Mr. Spellini smiled. "I hope so," he said. "She loves performing."

"Isn't she frightened by all the crowds?" Mandy said.

"Not at all," said Mr. Spellini. "She's used to it now."

Mandy frowned. "I'm worried that some of the animals in the play will be frightened," she said.

Mr. Spellini looked serious. "You must be sure that all the pets are able to stay close to their owners," he said. "That will give them confidence. It's also a good idea to have a quiet place backstage for them when they're not on-stage." He hesitated. "I could speak to Mrs. Garvie about the arrangements for the animals."

Mandy smiled. "Would you?" she said. "That would be great. It would be terrible if any of the pets got frightened. We have a pets rehearsal on Monday morning. All the animals will be there."

"Then I'll come on Monday as well," said Mr. Spellini.

Mandy smiled. "Thanks, Mr. Spellini," she said. "That would be terrific."

On Monday morning Mrs. Gavie took Mr. Spellini into her office for a long talk about the arrangements for the pets — and, of course, James's tricks. Then she gathered the cast of the play together for the pets rehearsal.

"We are very lucky to have a real magician to help us," she said to them. "Mr. Spellini is going to come to all our rehearsals — and he's going to teach James some magic tricks."

Amy Fenton jumped up and down. "Oh good," she said to James. "And then you can show us how they're done, James."

James shook his head, looking serious. "No, I can't," he said. "Mr. Spellini says I have to promise to keep the tricks secret."

Amy looked disappointed. But she soon brightened up. She had Minnie with her and she remembered she was going to do her whole gymnastic routine for the first time today. She was supposed to be the wizard's pet monkey and they all had to imagine her in a monkey costume.

Everybody cheered like crazy when Amy did her gymnastics. She was really good. She did some somersaults and backflips. She even did splits. She looked very proud when she finished.

Then it was Gary's turn with Gertie. But poor Gary just wasn't any good at the recorder.

"That doesn't matter," said Mr. Spellini. "Who *is* good at the recorder?"

Pam Stanton put her hand in the air. "I am,"

she said. "But I've got a part in the play already with Ginny, my guinea pig. And anyway, Gary really likes being the snake charmer."

"But Gary can still be the snake charmer," Mr. Spellini said to Pam. "You can play the recorder offstage while Gary mimes."

Gary looked puzzled. "But won't Gertie go looking for the music?"

Mr. Spellini shook his head. "You can't actually charm snakes, you know," he said gently. "But you could *pretend* you were charming Gertie. You could hold the recorder with one hand, lift Gertie up with the other, and sway as if she was dancing."

Gary's face lit up. "Oh, that's no problem. I'll be good at swaying. It's just the playing I'm bad at."

Everybody laughed. Except Amy. She had just looked down at Minnie's cage, which was sitting on a low table on the stage. It was empty.

"Minnie!" she said. "Oh, where's Minnie? She's escaped!"

"Oh, no!" said Richard Tanner. "I haven't

put Duchess back in her basket yet. Where is she?"

Mandy looked around the stage. "There, look!" she said as the Persian cat streaked across the floor. Mandy had never seen Duchess move so fast.

Something small and white scampered across the stage toward the curtain at the side.

"There's Minnie!" Amy wailed and the little girl made a dash for the corner of the stage.

Minnie ran up the curtain and on to the top of a piece of scenery. Duchess stood at the bottom, ready to spring. But before the cat could do anything, Amy scrambled up the wall, edged out along the scenery, and stretched out her hand toward Minnie.

Richard pounced on Duchess, scooped her into his arms, and put her back in her basket.

"Watch out, Amy!" Mrs. Garvie called.

But it was too late. The scenery toppled forward just as Amy grasped Minnie. Amy, Minnie, and the scenery came down with a crash.

Mandy was the first to reach them.

"Oh, is Minnie all right?" Amy said.

Mandy scooped up the little mouse before she could run off again and held her securely.

"I've got her. She's fine," she said. "What about you?"

Amy started to get to her feet. "I'm fine — ouch!" she said. "My ankle hurts!"

Mrs. Garvie arrived.

"Lie still, Amy," she said. "Are you all right?"

"Oh, my ankle," Amy wailed.

Mrs. Garvie felt Amy's ankle gently. Then she sat back with a sigh of relief.

"I don't think it's broken," she said. "But it's probably sprained. We'll have to get the nurse to take a look at you."

She looked at Amy and shook her head. "I'm afraid there won't be any gymnastics for you for a while, Amy," she said.

Amy looked up. Two big tears came into her eyes and spilled over.

"Oh, no!" she said. "And Minnie doesn't have a part, either."

Mandy looked down at the mouse, sitting

quietly in her hands. Minnie seemed fine after her adventure. Mandy put the little animal back in her cage.

"At least Minnie isn't hurt," Mandy said, trying to cheer Amy up.

Amy looked up at her and nodded. She was very white. Her ankle must be really painful.

"Oh, I know," she said. "I don't really mind as long as Minnie is all right. I'm just a bit disappointed, that's all. I was really looking forward to being in the play."

Mandy smiled and handed the cage to her. Amy was being very brave about all this. Mandy just wished she could wave James's magic wand and make her ankle better.

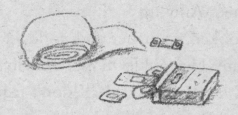

6

Spellini to the Rescue

The next week was really busy. There were rehearsals every day at school and every evening after dinner James went to Hobart's Corner to work with Mr. Spellini. And each day, James was looking more confident about his magic tricks.

So far he'd learned how to make a Ping-

Pong ball disappear from right under Mandy's nose and how to turn a box of torn-up newspaper into a whole page again just by tapping on the box with Mr. Spellini's wand. He was amazing!

Mandy had been to Hobart's Corner with James once or twice, but she hadn't been allowed to see how the tricks were done. Mr. Spellini was very serious about keeping the tricks a secret.

On Thursday, the two friends visited Amy after school. They found her sitting in a garden chair with her foot propped up in front of her and looking a bit miserable. Minnie's cage was on the grass beside her.

"Doctor Prescott says I can go back to school tomorrow," she said. "But I won't be able to do any gymnastics for *ages*."

Mandy and James sat down on the grass.

"Susan Davis is going to be the monkey now," Mandy said.

Amy nodded. "Susan is in my gymnastics class," she said. "She'll be really good."

"At least you'll be able to come and see the play," James said.

Amy sighed. "It isn't the same as being in it," she said unhappily. "But I'll cheer you all on, don't you worry."

Mandy bit her lip. Amy was trying hard to make the best of things. "How's Minnie?" she asked.

"Minnie is fine," said Amy. She looked at the white mouse running around its cage and tried to smile. "I thought maybe I would bring her to see the play."

James giggled. "Just make sure she doesn't get out of her cage and run around," he said. "Can you imagine Mrs. Ponsonby's face?"

Amy's smile got wider. "You bet I can," she said. "She'd be up on her chair, screeching the place down."

Mandy looked at Amy. Her eyes were dancing with mischief and she looked much more like her old self. If only she didn't have to miss out on being in the play.

But there was nothing they could do about that. *Or was there?* Sitting there, looking at Minnie running happily around in her cage, Mandy had an idea. She looked at her watch.

"Amy, we've got to go now," she said. "We're going to Hobart's Corner to see Mr. Spellini."

James got up as well. "We'll see you tomorrow at school," he said.

"Or sooner," said Mandy, and James looked at her in surprise. Amy didn't seem to notice.

"What do you mean sooner?" James said as they walked down the front path of Amy's house.

Mandy hurried him on. "Come on," she said. "I've got something to ask Mr. Spellini."

"What?" said James, running to keep up.

Mandy gave him a quick smile. "I know Amy can't be in the play," she said, "so we've just got to get Minnie into it instead!"

"But how will we manage to do that?" said James, running beside her.

"I don't know yet," said Mandy. "But we've got to try. I can't stand seeing Amy so unhappy. Especially when she's trying so hard to make the best of it. That's why I want to see Mr. Spellini."

James looked puzzled. "But what can he do?" he said.

Mandy shrugged and ran at the same time. "He's a magician, isn't he?" she said. "He'll be able to think of something."

Mr. Spellini gave them a huge smile as they arrived, panting, at Hobart's Corner. He was feeding his doves and Jack was helping him.

"Look!" called Jack as they both came racing across the grass. "The doves are eating out of my hand."

"Jack likes to feed them so much they're going to get too fat to fly," Mr. Spellini said, laughing.

"Whoops," said Jack. "Maybe I've given them enough."

"I think you have," said Mr. Spellini as Bianca fluttered up on to his shoulder.

"Let's put them back in their cage."

Jack, Mandy, and James helped shut them in — while Bianca peered down at them from Mr. Spellini's shoulder.

"How is she?" Mandy asked.

"She's terrific," the magician said. "I can't thank your mother enough, Mandy. Bianca is totally recovered."

Mandy smiled back and looked at the pretty white dove. She certainly looked well.

"She's the nicest dove I've ever seen," Mandy said.

"She likes to sit on my shoulder," said Jack

proudly. "Just the way she does with Mr. Spellini."

Mr. Spellini looked at Mandy and James closely.

"Something tells me you have something you want to talk to me about," he said.

James shook his head in wonder. "How did you know?" he said.

"Magic," said Mr. Spellini. "And the way you came rushing into the garden."

"Oh, Mr. Spellini, it's about Amy," Mandy said.

"That's the little girl who hurt her foot, isn't it?" said Mr. Spellini.

Mandy nodded. "She's so upset that she can't be in the play and neither can Minnie."

"Minnie?" said Mr. Spellini, puzzled.

"Her white mouse," said James.

Mr. Spellini rubbed his beard and looked thoughtful. "But what can I do?" he said.

"Well," said Mandy, "we thought that since you were a magician you might be able to do some magic for Amy."

"I can certainly do some tricks for her — to cheer her up," he said.

"Couldn't you use your magic to make her better?" asked Jack.

Mr. Spellini smiled. "That's something magicians can't do, Jack," he said. "I only wish I could."

"I thought maybe you could think of some way of getting Minnie into the play," said Mandy.

Mr. Spellini looked at Bianca. The dove ruffled her silky white feathers and put her head under her wing.

"I know how the little girl feels," Mr. Spellini said. "I was very upset when I thought I might not have Bianca in my act." He frowned. Then his face lit up. "James!" he said.

James looked up. "Yes?"

Mr. Spellini smiled and his eyes began to twinkle. "How would you like to do a trick with a mouse?" he asked.

James blinked and shoved his glasses up on his nose.

"A trick with an animal?" he said. "But I've only done tricks with cards and Ping-Pong balls and things."

Mr. Spellini nodded. "I know," he said. "But you really are getting quite good." He looked at Mandy. "We will have to give Mandy and Jack a special performance."

But Mandy wasn't listening. She was grinning with delight.

"You mean James could do a trick with Minnie? In the play?" she said.

"Perhaps," said Mr. Spellini. "We'll have to work out a trick and see if we can fit it into the story of the play."

Mandy bit her lip. "I hadn't thought of that," she said. "The play's finished and everybody knows their lines. We can't change it now."

"It isn't *quite* finished," James reminded her. "We still haven't decided what to do with Horrible Horace at the end."

Mandy swung around. "James, you're a genius!" she said. "That's it! That's the answer!"

"How?" said James.

Mandy's eyes were bright. "Don't you see?" she said. "Horrible Horace has to learn his lesson. He's been so horrible to everyone because he's bigger than everybody else. He's a great big bully. So at the end of the play he should get a dose of his own medicine. He needs to know what it feels like to be small and helpless."

She looked at James and Mr. Spellini. "You know, I think there *is* a part for Minnie in the play after all."

7

James the Magician

Mandy couldn't wait to tell Amy her idea. She rushed to the Fentons' house right after leaving Hobart's Corner. Amy was still in the garden. She was playing with Minnie, letting the little mouse run up and down her arm.

"I think she's feeling very left out," Mrs. Fenton said as she and Mandy watched Amy from the kitchen window.

"Just wait till I tell her my idea, Mrs. Fenton," Mandy said. "She'll feel better then, you'll see."

Mrs. Fenton looked at her in surprise. "What idea?" she said.

Mandy smiled. "We've found a way to include Minnie in the play!" she said to Amy's mother.

"Minnie?" said Mrs. Fenton. "But that would be wonderful." Then she smiled. "Come on," she said. "I think Amy should hear this first. Let's go and tell her."

Mandy ran out into the garden with Mrs. Fenton following behind her. Amy looked up, but she didn't smile. She was still really sad.

"Amy," said Mandy, "I've got a great surprise for you. Guess what? We've thought of a way to have Minnie in the play."

For a moment Amy didn't understand.

"Minnie?" she said. "What do you mean?"

Mandy sat down on the grass beside Amy

and started to explain the plan. Gradually Amy's face cleared and lit up with excitement as she listened.

"That's terrific," she said when Mandy had finished. She looked down at Minnie, curled in her lap. "Do you hear that, Minnie?" she said. "You're going to be in the play. You're going to be a star!"

Mandy grinned at Amy. "So can you come to Hobart's Corner tomorrow?" she said. She turned to Mrs. Fenton. "James is going to prac-

tice his tricks and Mr. Spellini needs to see Minnie. We need a little box for her — for the trick."

"I'll bring Amy over," Mrs. Fenton said. She looked at Amy and laughed. "I don't think I could stop her. I think she would hop all the way to Hobart's Corner if she had to."

Mandy smiled. Everything was working out.

James really did look like a wizard the next evening at Hobart's Corner. The suns and moons on his cape glittered in the early evening light and his pointy hat didn't fall off once during the whole practice. Underneath his cloak he had a white shirt with billowing sleeves, black trousers, and black shiny boots. What a wizard!

The garden at Hobart's Corner was filled with people. Mr. and Mrs. Gardiner were there, plus the Hunters, Grandma and Grandpa, Amy, Mandy, Jack, and Blackie. And of course, James, Mr. Spellini, and Minnie. Mr. Spellini's doves were perched in the apple tree.

James gave a great performance. First he did the trick with the Ping-Pong ball, making it disappear right in front of Grandma's eyes.

"Well, I never," said Grandma. "How did you do that?"

Then he got Grandpa to tear up a sheet of newspaper and place it in a wooden box. James tapped the box three times with his wand, then opened it — and there was a whole sheet of newspaper.

Grandpa laughed. "Honestly," he said, "I watched every move you made and I can't figure out how you did that."

"It's magic!" James said, taking a pack of cards from his pocket. "Now I'm going to do a card trick."

He asked Mandy to pick a card and put it back in the pack. Then he shuffled the cards and picked out Mandy's card.

"How did you know which card I picked?" she said.

James looked mysterious. "I can't tell you that," he said. "I'm sworn to secrecy."

Mr. Spellini nodded. "It wouldn't be magic if *everyone* could do it," he said.

Mandy smiled. James was so excited, his glasses kept sliding down his nose. He bit his lip in concentration, swirled around in his long black cloak, and produced a bunch of flowers from nowhere. He presented the flowers to Mrs. Gardiner.

"Oh, I wish I could grow flowers as easily as that," Grandma said and everybody laughed.

"Do a trick for *me*," said Jack.

James fanned the pack of cards, got Jack to pick a card and put it back, then threw the pack up in the air. Jack watched the cards fluttering down to earth. But Mandy has seen this trick before. She watched James. He took off his hat, tapped it with his magic wand — and Jack's card fell out!

"Wow!" said Jack.

"Bravo!" Mrs. Gardiner shouted as James pulled a string of scarves from behind his left ear and gave a final bow.

Mandy clapped loudly. "Your cloak looks great, Grandma," she said.

"And your hat looks great, too," said Grandma.

Mandy was pleased. She had worked hard on that pointy hat! Everybody clapped enthusiastically. Blackie ran around the garden, barking his head off. Then he came and leaped up on James, pawing at his cloak. The Labrador caught hold of something and tugged. It was a colored flag.

"Blackie! No! Bad boy!" James shouted as Blackie tugged harder.

Then Blackie was off across the garden with a long trail of colored flags flapping behind him. Mr. Spellini's doves fluttered higher up into the apple tree.

"I believe that's the end of the performance," Grandpa said, laughing.

James raced after Blackie, his cloak fluttering in the breeze. His hat fell off as he ran. Mr. Spellini picked it up and looked at it thoughtfully. Then he went over to his trunk and brought out a little box covered in silver paper. He turned to Amy.

"May I see Minnie?" he asked.

Amy took Minnie out of her cage and handed her to Mr. Spellini. Mr. Spellini took the little mouse carefully in his hands, clucking to her softly. Minnie twitched her whiskers. Then Mr. Spellini hummed and rocked Minnie slowly in his hands. She blinked a few times and closed her eyes.

Mandy and Amy watched with open mouths as Mr. Spellini put Minnie gently into the silver box.

"Perfect," he said. "I hoped I would have something in my trunk that would do."

"You put her to sleep," Amy said, her eyes wide. "How did you do that?"

Mr. Spellini looked at her and smiled. Mandy laughed.

"Don't tell us. Magic!" she said as James came back with the colored flags bunched in his hand.

"Sorry about that," he said, panting from the chase with Blackie.

Mr. Spellini had his head in the trunk again. He brought out a thing that looked like a big black paper clip. "Just what I need," he said.

Mandy peeked into the trunk. It was full of weird-shaped objects and mirrors and boxes.

"Now, James," said Mr. Spellini, "give me your hat and we'll start practicing the mouse trick. I've thought of a way to do it."

Amy looked at the magician. "Minnie will be safe?" she asked nervously.

Mr. Spellini stretched out a hand and at once a white dove swooped down from the apple tree and settled on his shoulder.

"It's Bianca!" Mandy said softly.

Mr. Spellini tipped the dove gently on to Amy's shoulder. Bianca fluttered her feathers slightly then found her balance. She settled close to Amy's neck and made a soft bubbly sound deep in her throat.

"Oooh! That's nice," said Amy, delighted.

Mr. Spellini smiled. "You take care of Bianca and I'll take care of Minnie," he said. "Is it a deal?"

Amy stretched up a hand and stroked Bianca's feathers. "It's a deal," she said.

Mr. Spellini looked thoughtful. "You know, James," he said, "I know you've got an apprentice. But every magician should have a proper assistant. What do you think? Would you like an assistant?"

James looked at Amy then he grinned at Mr. Spellini.

"I think an assistant would be a great idea," he said.

Amy looked up at Mr. Spellini. Her face broke into a wide smile.

"You mean me?" she said.

"You would feel better if you were James's assistant for the mouse trick," Mr. Spellini said. "Then you could be sure that Minnie was all right."

"What would I have to do?" asked Amy.

"Just stand beside James," said Mr. Spellini. "Of course, you would need a costume."

"A costume!" Amy said. "I'd love a costume. But there isn't time, is there?"

Mandy put her head to one side. "We could ask Grandma," she said. "She finished making my tunic for the play last night."

"Would she do it?" Amy asked.

"Why don't you go and see?" Mr. Spellini said. "James and I have work to do."

"Oh, can't we stay and watch?" said Mandy.

But Mr. Spellini shook his head.

"I know — magic secrets," Mandy said. But she didn't really mind.

"I want to go and ask about my costume," said Amy, pulling Mandy across the grass toward the house.

Mandy laughed. "You can hobble pretty fast when you want to, Amy," she said.

Amy turned a shining face to her. "I'm so excited," she said. "I really thought Minnie and I were going to be left out. Isn't this great?"

Mandy nodded. "Just wait and see what Grandma comes up with for a costume," she said. "That'll be great, too."

As they walked across the garden toward the house, Mandy looked back. James and Mr. Spellini were bent over the pointy hat, examining it closely. What were they up to, she wondered.

8

Star of the Show

"You look great!" Mandy said to Amy.

It was Saturday evening. Mandy and Amy were backstage waiting for the show to start. There were children everywhere. Those with pets had them safely secured in cages or traveling baskets.

"You look good, too. Your grandma is really

ace at making costumes," Amy said. "Nobody will guess what mine is made from."

Mandy nodded. There hadn't been much time to make anything complicated for Amy, but Mrs. Gardiner had found an old gold-colored curtain, which she and Grandma had made into a short swirly skirt with a little cape. Amy's hair was tied up with a big golden bow and she wore red boots to cover her bandage. She looked terrific.

Mandy, the wizard's apprentice, was wearing a bright green cap and a short red tunic over blue tights.

James was trying to stop Blackie from jumping up at him.

"It's the wand," he said. "He wants me to throw it for him."

"That's because of his part in the play," Mandy said.

She took Blackie by the collar and hauled him offstage. She dug her hands deep into the pocket of her tunic and brought out a couple of dog treats.

"That's bribery," said Pam Stanton, walking past with Ginny the guinea pig.

"It works," said Mandy as Blackie gobbled up the dog treats.

"There are thousands of people out there," Gary Roberts said, peering through a crack in the curtain. Gertie was draped around his neck.

Mandy came over and stood beside him. She gave Gertie a stroke. Then she saw the crowds.

"Wow!" she said. "All of Welford has turned up."

Gary laughed. "Look at Mrs. Ponsonby," he said. "She's right in the front row."

Mandy looked. Mrs. Ponsonby was sitting up straight in her chair, talking loudly to anybody who would listen.

"She's told the whole village that Mr. Spellini is a dangerous spy," Jill Redfern said behind them.

Mandy turned around. Jill was giving Toto's shell a final polish.

"Doesn't he look great?" she said.

Mandy looked around. *Everybody* looked

great. Gary had a big blue turban on his head, Amy sparkled and shone in her gold costume, and James looked just like a wizard in his tall hat, cloak, and wand. Andrew was like a real villain, dressed up as Horace, all in black. He looked really sinister — a truly frightening giant!

Mrs. Garvie clapped her hands softly. "Off the stage now," she said. "We're almost ready to begin." She looked around at all her pupils. "What is it they say in the theater? Break a leg!"

Amy looked down at her foot. "I nearly did that already," she said.

Everybody laughed and Mrs. Garvie herded them off the stage. She put her fingers to her lips and pressed a button on the tape recorder at the side of the stage. At the same time the lights dimmed.

The music began and then the curtains slowly opened. The first batch of children ran on to the stage with their pets and the show began.

The group of children were acting as villagers at a carnival. There were all sorts of performers. There was dancing and singing and finally all the villagers did a conga around the stage.

Then Gary sat in the middle of the stage, holding Gertie up while Pam played the recorder backstage. Gary and Gertie were a great success. All the villagers cheered and brought their pets closer to see the fun.

But, as they gathered around Gary, a black figure appeared at the back of the stage. It was Horrible Horace. The villagers fell back in fear as Horace walked around. He snatched Toto the tortoise from Jill and told the villagers what he wanted. If the villagers did not work for him and do everything he said, he would kill Toto — and all the animals in the village.

Horace marched to the front of the stage and growled at the audience. Behind him, the villagers huddled together, wondering what to do.

Mandy, James, and Susan were waiting in the wings.

"This is it," said James.

"I'm really nervous," Susan Davis said, putting on her monkey mask.

"You were great at rehearsal," James reassured her. He looked at Mandy. "Ready?"

Mandy nodded. "Good luck," she whispered. She looked down at Blackie, standing beside Mrs. Garvie. "It'll be your turn soon, Blackie," she said softly.

"You're on now," Mrs. Garvie said, holding Blackie close to her side.

Mandy and James walked out on to the stage with Susan tumbling around them.

"Oh, Master," Mandy said in a clear voice. "This is a fine carnival. But nobody is having any fun. Why don't you show them some magic tricks?"

From then on Mandy hardly had time to think. Everything worked perfectly. The villagers started having fun again. With the wizard's help, they all ganged up on Horace and tied him up. Pam played the recorder offstage while Gary swayed about so much his turban wobbled. Jack's and Laura's rabbits received loud applause, and each time Horrible Horace snarled and hissed the audience booed and hissed back. Susan, the wizard's monkey, did her gymnastics, tumbling around the stage to loud applause. But it was James and his magic tricks that got the loudest cheers. He was wonderful.

The play went so fast Mandy could hardly believe it when the last scene came.

Horrible Horace had escaped. He was standing center stage and the villagers were cowering in front of him, afraid of him once again. He had stolen the wizard's magic wand and he was going to do something horrible to all the animals. The wizard lay helpless at Horrible Horace's feet. Without his wand, he had no power left. Horrible Horace lifted up the wand and waved it.

This was Blackie's cue. Mandy walked on from the wings with Blackie at her side.

"Look what you have done to my master!" she cried. "You have stolen his wand. You have stolen his power!"

Horace raised the wizard's magic wand higher.

"And now I'm going to turn all your pets to stone," he snarled.

Mandy knelt down center stage, right next to James.

"Go, Blackie! Get Andrew!" she whispered to Blackie. "Fetch the stick!"

Blackie didn't need to be told twice. He made a dive for Horrible Horace and started chasing him around the stage. Horrible Horace threw the wand high into the air and Blackie leaped for it.

Mandy held her breath. Blackie caught the wand and turned to take it back to Andrew.

Mandy rattled the box of dog biscuits in her pocket and Blackie stopped and looked at her.

"Here, boy. Here, Blackie," she whispered.

Blackie put his head to one side and for a moment Mandy thought he wasn't going to come to her. Then he galloped across the stage, put the wand down at Mandy's feet, and wagged his tail.

"Good boy!" Mandy whispered and gave him a biscuit. There were laughs from the audience as he chomped it noisily.

Mandy put the wand into James's hand and stood up.

"Abracadabra, hubble and bubble, the wizard's wand will solve this trouble!" she said in a loud voice.

At once James leaped to his feet. The Wizard of Welford had gotten back his power. All the villagers cheered. Then they all went silent again as Horrible Horace started to walk toward James.

Mandy held her breath. Now it was time for the best trick of all. Amy was standing beside James. She had a small round object in her hand. Horrible Horace paced steadily toward James. Then James waved his wand three times. He twirled round, his cloak billowing behind him.

Just at that moment, Amy threw something down on the stage. There was a puff of smoke and Mandy saw Andrew dive offstage under the cover of James's cloak and the smoke. James twirled again and swept his pointy hat off his head.

Mandy watched closely. She saw James reach inside the hat and there was the silver box. In a moment he had the box open and held Minnie up for everyone to see. The Wizard of Welford had turned Horrible Horace into a mouse!

It was terrific. The villagers on the stage cheered, and the audience cheered. Amy looked as if she would do a cartwheel in spite of her ankle. And, above them all, held in James's hand, was Minnie. The little mouse blinked in the bright lights and twitched her long whiskers.

All eyes were on the little mouse. She really was the star of the show.

"Horrible Horace will never bully the village again," James announced. "I have cast a spell on him — a spell to turn him into a tiny helpless little animal. The animals of Welford are safe!"

Then the curtain came down. They had to take five bows. Everybody was on their feet stamping and cheering. Finally Mrs. Garvie had to come on and ask everyone to sit down.

"Mr. Spellini is going to give us a very special treat," she said. "I think everybody knows how helpful he has been with the play."

There was clapping from the audience and Mrs. Garvie held up her hand again until it died down.

"Mr. Spellini has agreed to give a magic performance just for us," she said. She turned to the side of the stage and announced. "Ladies and gentlemen, the Spectacular Spellini!"

Mandy, James, and Amy sat down on the stage with all the other children. Everyone had their pets beside them, safely back in their baskets and cages. Blackie lay contentedly between Mandy and James, wagging his tail.

Mr. Spellini began his act. He was amazing. He took three silver balls out of Pam Stanton's mouth. He turned Gary's turban into a beach ball. He made Andrew Pearson disappear entirely. He even smashed Mrs. Garvie's watch with a big golden hammer — and gave it back to her without a mark on it.

"He's terrific," said James. He grinned at Mandy. "He's the *real* Wizard of Welford."

"Oh, he's finished!" said Amy.

Mandy looked at the stage. Mr. Spellini was

bowing to the audience. Then he threw out his arms and his doves came fluttering down from the rafters above the stage. They settled along his outstretched arms, ruffling their feathers and cooing. Mandy spotted Bianca. The white dove walked up Mr. Spellini's arm and settled in her favorite place on his shoulder.

The performance was over. It had all been wonderful. Mr. Spellini turned to look at Mandy. He gave her a wink and raised his arms. The doves circled the stage above Mr. Spellini's

head as he swept his hat off. He took a huge bunch of flowers out of his hat and threw them right over the stage toward Mrs. Ponsonby. Mrs. Ponsonby was so surprised, she threw up her hands with a squeak of alarm — and caught them.

Mandy heard Mrs. Ponsonby say, "Well, really!"

Then she looked at the flowers. She stood up and took a bow as well.

"Honestly, Mrs. Ponsonby's got some nerve," said James.

"Who cares?" said Amy softly, stroking the little mouse. "Minnie is a star. It's magic!"

Mandy nodded happily. "Magic," she repeated. Then she looked at Minnie. "It's mouse magic!"